IDALIA'S
Project ABC

Proyecto ABC

An Urban Alphabet Book
in English and Spanish

by Idalia Rosario

Henry Holt and Company / New York

For my son, David Kim,
Jessica, Dawn, April and Lenore,
and for all of us
who grew up in "los proyectos."

Special thanks to Sal Artale, Carmen Puigdollers,
Joe Quiñones, Eddy, Ernesto, Jenny, Rick,
Lala Torres, and Miriam Chaikin. Without their help
and love this book could never have been.

Note:
Bloque es un anglicismo para la palabra cuadra.
Elevador es un anglicismo para la palabra ascensor.
Polución es un anglicismo para la palabra contaminación.

Note: The Spanish Alphabet has three letters more than the
English. The letters **ch**, **ll** and **ñ** do not exist in English.

Copyright © t981 by Idalia Rosario
All rights reserved, including the right to reproduce
this book or portions thereof in any form.
Published by Henry Holt and Company, Inc., 115 West 18th Street, New York, New York 10011.
Distributed in Canada by Fitzhenry & Whiteside Limited, 195 Allstate Parkway, Markham, Ontario L3R 4T8.
Library of Congress Cataloging in Publication Data
Rosario, Idalia.   Idalia's Project ABC. English and Spanish.
SUMMARY: Introduces the alphabet by means of brief bilingual descriptions of city life.
1. Spanish language—Readers—City and town life—New York (City)   2. City and town life—New York (City)—
Juvenile literature.   [1. Spanish language—Alphabet.   2. Spanish language—Readers.   3. City and town life.
4. Alphabet]   I. Title.
PC4115.R69   468.6′421   80-21013

ISBN 0-8050-0286-3 (hardcover)
10   9   8   7   6   5   4   3   2
ISBN 0-8050-0296-0 (paperback)
10   9   8   7   6   5   4   3   2

Printed in the United States of America

Aa is for asking. Asking Papo's mother
if he could come out to play.

Aa es para amigo. Le pregunto a la mamá
de mi amigo Papo si puede salir a jugar.

Bb is for bricks. Projects and tenements are built with bricks.

Bb es para bloque. En el bloque donde vivo, los edificios están hechos de ladrillos.

Cc is for cement. Our city sidewalks are made of cement.

Cc es para cemento. En nuestra ciudad las aceras están hechas de cemento.

Ch ch es para chimenea. Algunos edificios y fábricas tienen chimeneas.

(*Chimenea* means chimney: Some buildings and factories have chimneys.)

Dd is for David. My little brother David likes to dance "la salsa."

Dd es para David. A mi hermanito David le gusta bailar la salsa.

Ee is for elevator to the eleventh floor.

Ee es para elevador. Yo subo en el elevador hasta el piso once.

Ff is for fun, the fun my friends and I have when the fire hydrants are open.

Ff es para fiesta, la fiesta que hacemos cuando abrimos la bomba de agua.

Gg is for graffiti,
the writing on the walls.

Gg es para el "graffiti" que pintamos en las paredes.

Hh is for housing development, a fancy name for the projects where I live.

Hh es para hogar. Mi hogar está en el caserío.

Ii is for incinerator, where we put the garbage.

Ii es para incinerador. El incinerador es donde ponemos la basura.

Jj is for Joe. The janitor works hard to keep our building clean.

Jj es para José. Él es el hombre que trabaja limpiando el edificio.

Kk is for karate. My friend Quincy knows karate.

Kk es para karate. Mi amigo Quincy estudia karate.

Ll is for litter. We helped clean the litter in the empty lot.

Ll es para limpieza. Muchos solares vacíos necesitan limpieza.

LI ll es para la lluvia.
La lluvia no me deja salir,
pero ayuda a las plantas
a crecer en la ciudad.

(*Lluvia* means rain: The rain keeps us in,
but it helps the plants to grow in the city.)

Mm is for market, where we go to buy food.

Mm es para el mercado. En el mercado compramos muchos alimentos.

Nn is for Nana. She is my nice grandma who always calls me "Negrita."

Nn es para Nana. Ella es mi querida abuelita que siempre me llama Negrita.

Ññ es para ñame. A mí papá le gusta cocinar ñames y nosotros ayudamos.

(*Ñame* means yams: My father likes to cook yams and we like to help.)

Oo is for open.
I always look
through the peephole
before I open
the front door.

Oo es para observar.
Antes de abrir
la puerta, miro
por la mirilla
para observar
quién toca.

Pp is for the island of Puerto Rico.

Pp es para la isla de Puerto Rico.

Qq is for Quincy. Quincy lent me his lantern when there was a blackout in the city.

Qq es para Quincy. Quincy me prestó su quinqué

Rr is for rats. Rats are a health hazard for all cities.

Rr es para las ratas. Las ratas son un peligro en todas las ciudades.

Ss is for sounds. The city is full of different sounds.

Ss es para sonidos. La ciudad está llena de sonidos diferentes.

Tt is for train. Sometimes we take a trip on the train.

Tt es para el tren. A veces viajamos en el tren.

Uu is for unity. Although my friends are different, we play in unity.

Uu es para unidad. Nosotros, aunque somos diferentes, jugamos todos unidos.

Vv is for vacation. During the summer vacation,
my grandparents come from Puerto Rico to visit me in New York.

**Vv es para vacaciones. En las vacaciones del verano,
mis abuelitos vienen a visitarme a Nueva York.**

Ww is for Wilma. Someday I'd like to be an artist like Quincy's sister Wilma.

Ww es para Wilma. Algún día voy a ser artista como Wilma, la hermana de Quincy.

Xx is for Xiomara. Ana's mother, Xiomara, passed out leaflets against pollution in our neighborhood.

Xx es para Xiomara. Xiomara, la mamá de Ana, repartió hojas sueltas en contra de la polución del aire.

Yy is for you. Now that you know so much about me...
would you like to visit me? Say yes!

Yy es para ya. Ahora que ya sabes tantas
cosas sobre mí... ¿querrias visitarme? ¡Di que sí!

Zz is for zoo. Now I'd like to read about the zoo. Me too!

Zz es para el parque zoológico. Ahora me gustaria leer sobre el zoológico. ¡A mí también!